Published by
North Atlantic Books
P.O. Box 12327
Berkeley, California 94712

Cover art and design by Linda L. Knoll
Book design by Linda L. Knoll and Brad Greene
Printed in the United States of America

Patient for Pumpkins is sponsored by the Society for the Study of Native Arts and Sciences, a nonprofit educational corporation whose goals are to develop an educational and cross-cultural perspective linking various scientific, social, and artistic fields; to nurture a holistic view of arts, sciences, humanities, and healing; and to publish and distribute literature on the relationship of mind, body, and nature.

North Atlantic Books' publications are available through most bookstores. For further information, visit our website at www.northatlanticbooks.com or call 800-733-3000.

Library of Congress Cataloging-in-Publication Data

Knoll, Linda L.
    Patient for pumpkins / Linda L. Knoll.
        pages cm
    Summary: In weekly trips to the farmers' market with his father, a boy learns about seasonal fruits and vegetables, and about patience.
    ISBN 978-1-58394-708-1 (hardback)
    [1. Farmers' markets—Fiction. 2. Vegetables—Fiction. 3. Fruits—Fiction. 4. Pumpkin—Fiction. 5. Patience—Fiction.] I. Title.
    PZ7.K749Pat 2014
    [E]—dc23

Qualibre/CG, North Mankato, MN, Jan 2014, Job #113
1 2 3 4 5 6 7 8 9 Qualibre/CG 19 18 17 16 15 14

Patient for Pumpkins

Story and Illustrations by Linda L. Knoll

North Atlantic Books
Berkeley, California

It's springtime and my dad is
taking me to the farmers' market.
I can't wait! I'm going to get a
pumpkin. It will be giant and round
and orange and perfect!

Music is playing and people crowd the street. As we look down the row of tents, I search for the pumpkins.

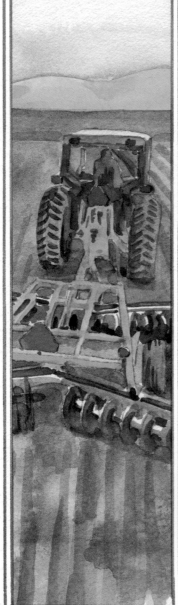
Blueberries, broccoli, blackberries, and artichokes. Sweet strawberries! Farmers say hello and give us samples to taste.

"But where are the pumpkins?"

"It's only May," says Dad. "Be patient."

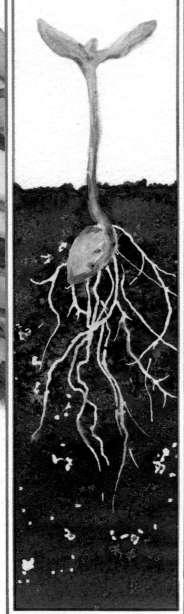

*At the farm,
the pumpkin
seeds are planted
in the ground.
In a few days the
seed breaks open
and roots begin
to grow.*

We're going back to the farmers' market today.
We buy apricots, asparagus, cherries, and
a big bunch of flowers for mom.

The vines grow quickly and send out curly tendrils.

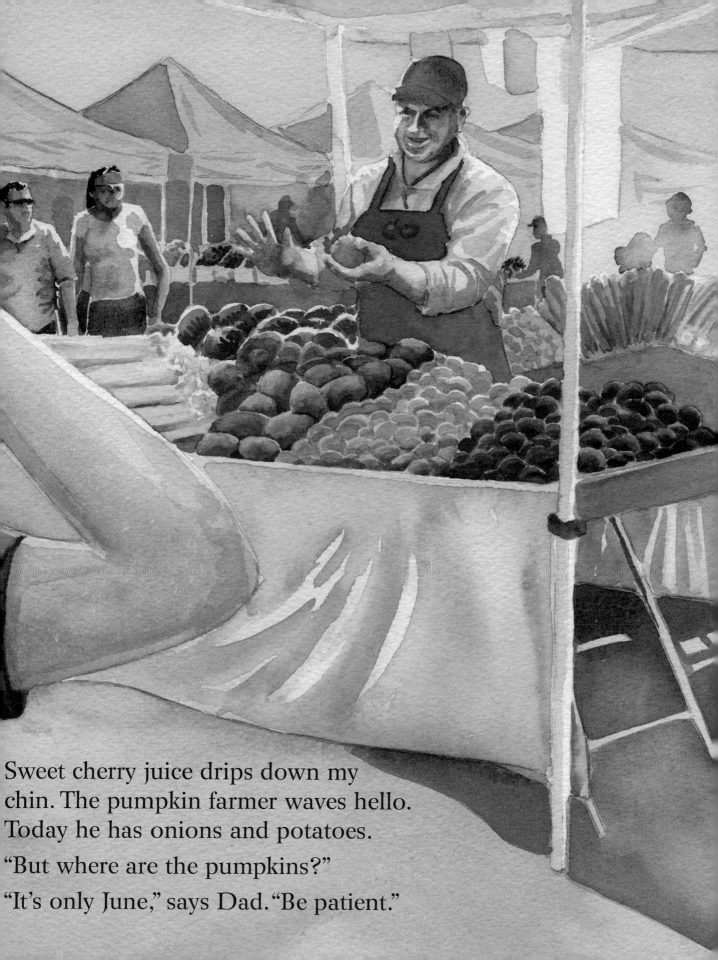

Sweet cherry juice drips down my
chin. The pumpkin farmer waves hello.
Today he has onions and potatoes.

"But where are the pumpkins?"

"It's only June," says Dad. "Be patient."

What should we buy for our Fourth of July picnic? The market is bigger now. Local farmers are bringing different fruits and vegetables every week. The blueberries are gone, but we buy lots of other yummy things.

The pumpkin plants blossom, and bees help to pollinate the flowers.

Plums, peaches, plump tomatoes, and corn!

Dad buys me a big slice of cold watermelon.
"But where are the pumpkins?"
"It's only July," says Dad. "Be patient."

The blossoms turn into tiny green pumpkins.

August is SO hot! Dad takes me to the market in the morning while it's still cool.

The large leaves protect the pumpkins from the hot sun.

Persimmons, purple peppers, eggplants, and beets.
"What are those?" I ask my dad.

Peppers

"Brussels sprouts," he says.
"They're like little cabbages."
"But where are the pumpkins?"
"It's only August," says Dad.
"Be patient."

It's the start of September. But still no pumpkins. Dad explains that fruits and vegetables come and go with the seasons. Some things, like blueberries, ripen quickly and only last a few weeks. But other things need more time.

By the end of September, the pumpkins finally turn orange.

Pears and pomegranates. Almonds and cheese.
"But where are the pumpkins?"
"September is almost over," says Dad. "Pumpkins
can't be hurried. They'll be here soon."

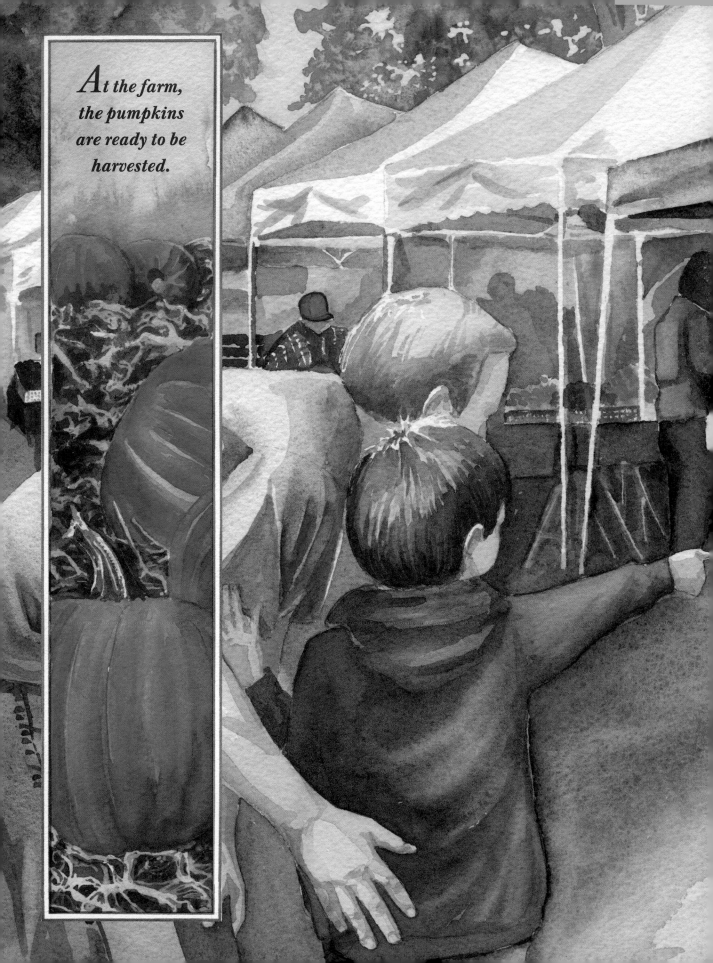

At the farm, the pumpkins are ready to be harvested.

October is here. The morning air is crisp and cool.
The leaves are turning golden yellow and fiery red.
Then I see them. Beautiful, big, orange pumpkins
glowing in the morning sun.

The farmer brings the pumpkins to the market.

Awesome! Fantastic! Beautiful!
But which one will I choose?

There are many different kinds of pumpkins. Some are very small, and some grow very large.

They all look so different. I see a short,
bluish one that looks funny. Then dad picks
up a tall bumpy one that's strange too.

Finally, I find a humongous bright orange pumpkin that's not too short, and not too tall. It's so big, the farmer lends us a wheelbarrow to carry it.

After the harvest, the farmer plows the dead vines back into the soil. The plants give the dirt nutrients that will make it ready for planting next spring.

When we get home, Mom says, "Wow, that's the perfect pumpkin."

"When can I carve it?" I ask.

"How about right now?"

Do you shop at your farmers' market?
Check off the fruits and vegetables you have tried!
Then try some new ones!

- ❏ almond
- ❏ apple
- ❏ apricot
- ❏ artichoke
- ❏ arugula
- ❏ asparagus
- ❏ avocado
- ❏ basil
- ❏ beet
- ❏ bell pepper
- ❏ blackberry
- ❏ blueberry
- ❏ bok choy
- ❏ boysenberry
- ❏ broccoli
- ❏ brussels sprouts
- ❏ cabbage
- ❏ cantaloupe
- ❏ carrot
- ❏ cauliflower
- ❏ celery
- ❏ chard
- ❏ cherry
- ❏ chili pepper
- ❏ cilantro
- ❏ corn

- ❏ cucumber
- ❏ eggplant
- ❏ fava bean
- ❏ fig
- ❏ garlic
- ❏ ginger
- ❏ grape
- ❏ grapefruit
- ❏ green bean
- ❏ kale
- ❏ kiwi
- ❏ kumquat
- ❏ leek
- ❏ lemon
- ❏ lemongrass
- ❏ lettuce
- ❏ loquat
- ❏ melon
- ❏ mushroom
- ❏ mustard green
- ❏ nectarine
- ❏ olive
- ❏ okra
- ❏ onion
- ❏ orange
- ❏ peach

- ❏ pea
- ❏ pear
- ❏ persimmon
- ❏ pistachio
- ❏ plum
- ❏ pluot
- ❏ pomegranate
- ❏ potato
- ❏ pumpkin
- ❏ quince
- ❏ radish
- ❏ raspberry
- ❏ spinach
- ❏ squash
- ❏ strawberry
- ❏ swiss chard
- ❏ tangerine
- ❏ taro
- ❏ tomatillo
- ❏ tomato
- ❏ turnip
- ❏ walnut
- ❏ watermelon
- ❏ yam
- ❏ zucchini

Some other locally produced products you might find at your farmers' market:

- ❏ arts & crafts
- ❏ bread
- ❏ cheese
- ❏ desserts
- ❏ eggs
- ❏ herbs & spices
- ❏ honey
- ❏ meat
- ❏ olive oil
- ❏ nuts
- ❏ plants & flowers
- ❏ popcorn
- ❏ sauces
- ❏ soaps